BEARCUB BIOS

RUTH BADER GINSBURG

SUPREME COURT JUSTICE

by Rachel Rose

Consultant: Beth Gambro
Reading Specialist, Yorkville, Illinois

BEARPORT PUBLISHING

Minneapolis, Minnesota

Teaching Tips

BEFORE READING

- Discuss what a biography is. What kinds of things might a biography tell a reader?
- Look through the glossary together. Read and discuss the words.
- Go on a picture walk, looking through the pictures to discuss vocabulary and make predictions about the text.

DURING READING

- Encourage readers to point to each word as it is read. Stop occasionally to ask readers to point to a specific word in the text.
- If a reader encounters an unknown word, ask them to look at the rest of the page. Are there any clues to help them understand?

AFTER READING

- Check for understanding.
  - Where did Ruth Bader Ginsburg grow up?
  - What does she do?
  - What does she care about?
- Ask the readers to think deeper.
  - If you met Ruth, what question would you like to ask her? Why?

Credits:
Cover and title page, © Supreme Court of the United States/Public Domain and © Steven Frame/Shutterstock; 3, © Rob Crandall/Shutterstock; 5, © KORT DUCE/Getty Images; 7, rSnapshotPhotos/Shutterstock; 8, © Lewis Liu/Shutterstock; 11, © Bettmann/Getty Images; 13, © Lynn Gilbert/Wikimedia Commons; 14 © Courtesy Columbia Law School; 16-17, © Diana Walker/Getty Images; 19, © Alex Wong/Getty Images; 20-21, © WENN Rights Ltd/Alamy Stock Photo; 22, © Rob Crandall/Shutterstock; 23TL, © Steve Petteway, Staff Photographer of the Supreme Court; 23TC, © simpson33/iStock; 23TR, © VP Photo Studio/Shutterstock; 23BL, © MTMCOINS iStock; and 23BR, © Bill Chizek/iStock.

Library of Congress Cataloging-in-Publication Data

Names: Rose, Rachel, 1968– author. Title: Ruth Bader Ginsburg : Supreme Court justice / by Rachel Rose. Description: Minneapolis, Minnesota : Bearport Publishing Company, 2021. | Series: Bearcub bios | Includes bibliographical references and index. Identifiers: LCCN 2020000559 (print) | LCCN 2020000560 (ebook) | ISBN 9781642809824 (library binding) | ISBN 9781642809930 (paperback) | ISBN 9781647470043 (ebook) Subjects: LCSH: Ginsburg, Ruth Bader—Juvenile literature. | United States. Supreme Court—Biography—Juvenile literature. Classification: LCC KF8745.G56 . R67 2020 (print) | LCC KF8745.G56 (ebook) | DDC 347.73/2634 [B]—dc23 LC record available at https://lccn.loc.gov/2020000559 LC ebook record available at https://lccn.loc.gov/2020000560

Copyright © 2021 Bearport Publishing Company. All rights reserved. No part of this publication may be reproduced in whole or in part, stored in any retrieval system, or transmitted in any form or by any means, electronic, mechanical, photocopying, recording, or otherwise, without written permission from the publisher.

For more information, write to Bearport Publishing, 5357 Penn th, Minneapolis, MN 55419.

Printed nited States of America.

Contents

On the Highest Court 4

Ruth's Life 6

Did You Know?........................ 22

Glossary 23

Index 24

Read More 24

Learn More Online..................... 24

About the Author 24

On the Highest Court

Ruth Bader Ginsburg raised her hand.

She promised to follow the **law**.

She was becoming a top judge!

5

Ruth's Life

Ruth grew up in New York.

She looked up to her mother, Celia.

Celia helped Ruth learn to be strong.

New York

Ruth and Marty went to school here.

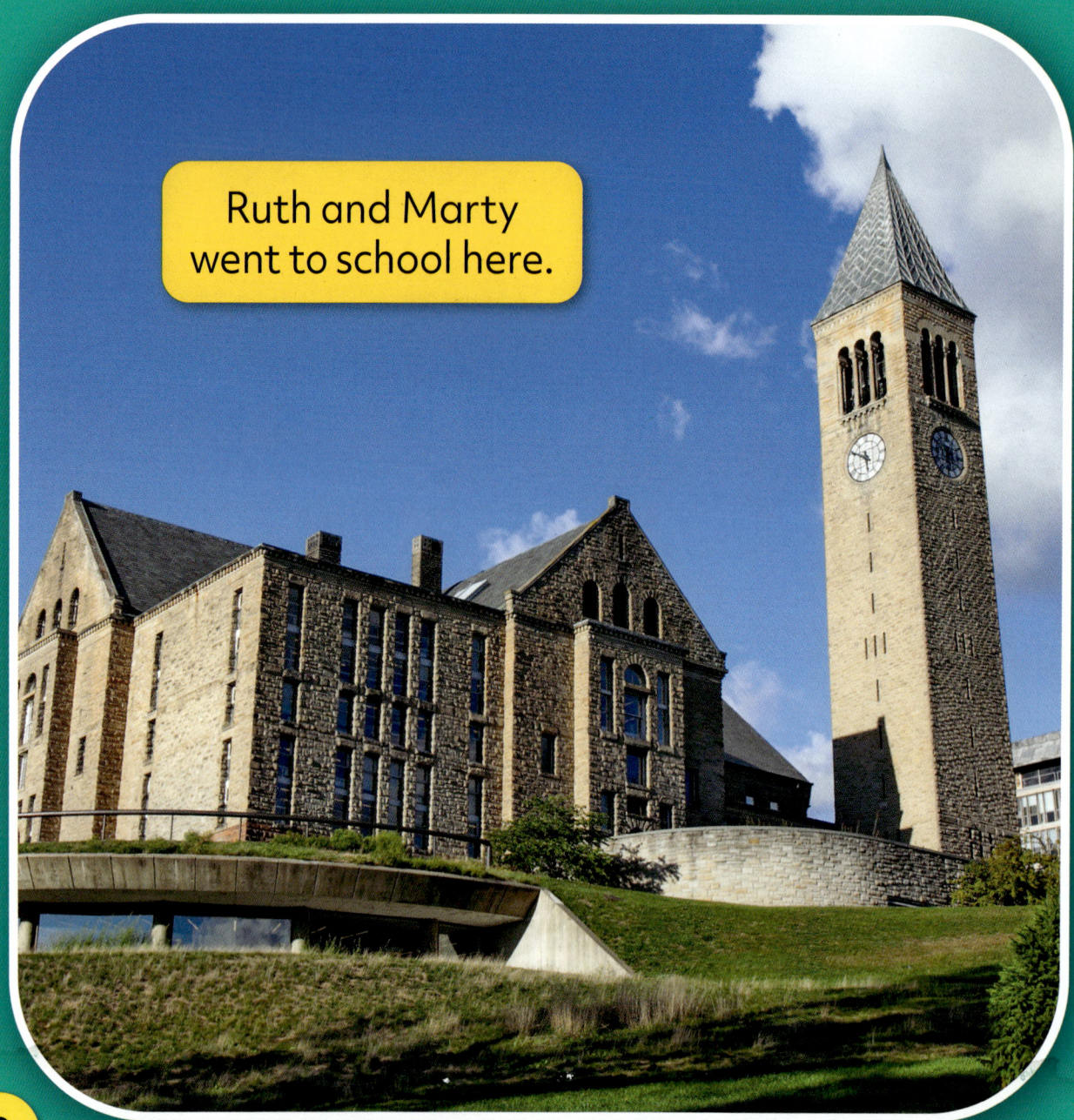

Growing up, Ruth loved to read.

She was very smart.

Ruth met her husband, Marty, when they were in college.

After college, Ruth learned about law.

There were mostly men at her school.

She was the best in her class!

11

It was hard for Ruth to find a job.

Not many people wanted women **lawyers**.

Finally, she started working for a judge.

13

14

Ruth had many jobs.

She was a law teacher.

Then, she was a judge.

In her work, Ruth cared about things being fair for women.

In 1993, Ruth became a **justice** on the **Supreme Court**.

She was the second woman ever on the court.

She heard about many problems.

Ruth

17

Ruth learned about a **military** school.

Women were not allowed to go there.

Ruth knew this was not fair.

She said the school had to let women in, too.

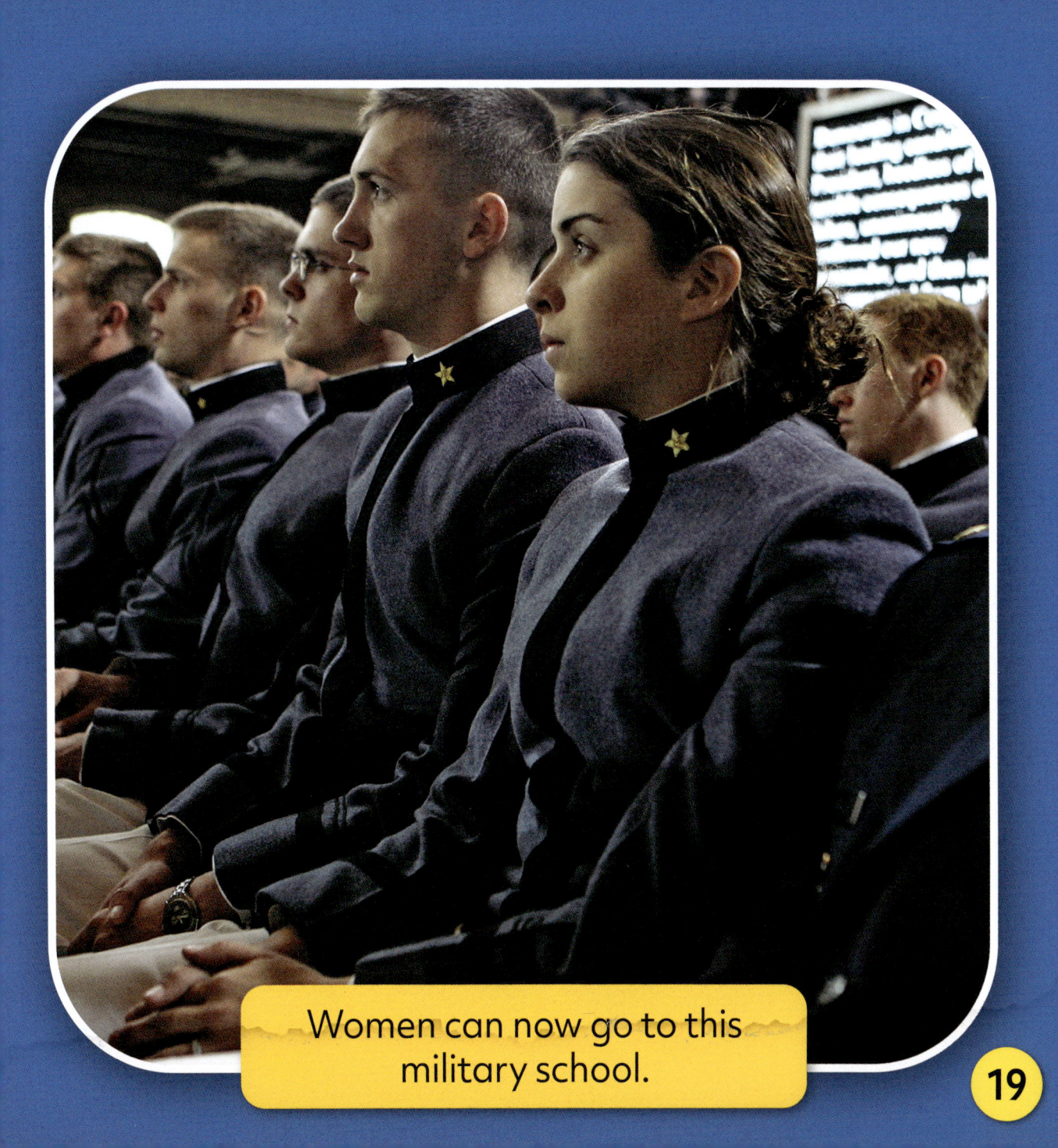

Women can now go to this military school.

20

Ruth is still working hard.

She works for everyone.

And she plans to keep going!

Did You Know?

Born: March 15, 1933

Family: Celia (mother), Nathan (father)

When she was a kid: She loved to read Nancy Drew books.

Special fact: Ruth is a very bad cook! Her husband made all the family meals.

Ruth says: "Fight for the things that you care about, but do it in a way that will lead others to join you."

Life Connections

No matter how hard things got for Ruth, she kept going. Have you had hard times in your life? What helps you to keep going?

Glossary

justice a judge on the Supreme Court

law the rules of a place

lawyers people whose job it is to help others with law problems

military having to do with armies or war

Supreme Court the highest court in the United States

Index

Celia 6, 22
judge 4, 12, 15
justice 16
lawyer 12
New York 6
school 8, 10, 18–19
Supreme Court 16

Read More

Calkhoven, Laurie. *Ruth Bader Ginsburg (You Should Meet).* New York: Simon Spotlight (2019).

Scirri, Kaitlin. *Ruth Bader Ginsburg: Supreme Court Justice (Barrier-Breaker Bios).* New York: Cavendish Square (2019).

Learn More Online

1. Go to **www.factsurfer.com**
2. Enter "**Ruth Bader Ginsburg**" into the search box.
3. Click on the cover of this book to see a list of websites.

About the Author

Rachel Rose lives in San Francisco. She grew up in Ireland, where her father was a lawyer.